Charles Dickens

A CHRISTMAS CAROL

Retold by
I.M. Richardson
Illustrated by
Jane Kendall

Troll Associates

Library of Congress Cataloging in Publication Data

    Charles Dickens' A Christmas carol.

    Summary: A retelling of the story about a miser whose
life is changed by Christmas.
    [1. Christmas—Fiction.   2. Ghosts—Fiction.
3. England—Fiction]   I. Kendall, Jane F., ill.
II. Dickens, Charles, 1812-1870.   Christmas carol.
III. Title.
PZ7.R3948Ch   1988   [E]   87-11270
ISBN 0-8167-1053-8 (lib. bdg.)
ISBN 0-8167-1054-6 (pbk.)
10 9 8 7 6 5 4 3 2

Once upon a Christmas Eve, Ebenezer Scrooge sat in his office. His partner, Jacob Marley, had died. But Scrooge was stingy and mean enough for both of them. He was too cheap to put another lump of coal on the fire, so the office was as cold as ice. Scrooge's clerk, Bob Cratchit, shivered as he worked.

Suddenly Scrooge's jolly nephew came in and invited the old man to Christmas dinner.

"Bah! Humbug!" said Scrooge. "What good has Christmas ever done for you?"

The nephew replied, "Why, Christmas is the only time I know of when people open their hearts and spread love and kindness everywhere. So although it has never put gold in my pocket, I believe Christmas is a wonderful time."

Bob Cratchit put down his pen and clapped his hands. But when Scrooge glared at him, he got back to his work at once.

As Scrooge's nephew left, he called back, "Well, Merry Christmas anyway, Uncle! And Happy New Year, too!"

Before long, a fat gentleman entered the office. "I am seeking donations for the poor," he said. "The homeless have nowhere to go on Christmas."

"Are there no prisons?" asked Scrooge. "Are there no workhouses?"

The man replied, "Many would rather die than go to those places."

"If they are going to die," snapped Scrooge, "then they had better do it and decrease the surplus population. Good day, sir!"

At closing time, Scrooge said to his clerk, "I suppose you'll want the day off tomorrow, Cratchit! Bah! I don't care if it is Christmas. It's a poor excuse for picking a man's pocket every twenty-fifth of December! Well, be here all the earlier the next day!" Then he shut out the lights and went home.

That evening, Scrooge was sitting by a small fire in his bedroom when he heard the sound of clanking chains. The noise grew louder, and suddenly he was face to face with the ghost of Jacob Marley.

"I must wander forever, dragging the things I loved in life," said the ghost, holding up a heavy cashbox that was chained to his waist. "But you can escape my fate. You will be haunted by three spirits—the ghosts of Christmas Past, Present, and Future. Heed them well."

When Marley's ghost had left, Scrooge started to say "Humbug!" but he did not finish the word. He went to bed and fell asleep at once.

He awoke as the chimes struck. A hand drew back the bed curtains, and Scrooge stared at the first spirit.

"I am the Ghost of Christmas Past," said the spirit. "Rise, and walk with me."

Scrooge touched the spirit's robe and suddenly found himself at the boarding school where he had lived as a boy. On Christmas vacation, when his friends had gone home, young Scrooge had been left alone at the school. Now Scrooge saw himself, sitting in a lonely corner, and he sighed, "Poor boy."

Next they were at Fezziwig's warehouse, where Scrooge had served as an apprentice. It was Christmas Eve, and Fezziwig was giving a party. Everyone—including young Scrooge—was singing, dancing, and having fun. As Scrooge watched, the spirit said, "A small matter, to make these poor folks so happy." And Scrooge thought about how miserably he had treated his own clerk, Bob Cratchit.

The scene changed, and Scrooge saw someone he had loved long ago. She had once said to him, "You have changed, Ebenezer. Nothing matters to you anymore, except money. So we must go our separate ways."

Now that same girl was married and surrounded by happy children. Her husband came through the door, bringing toys and presents for everyone. After the presents had been opened and the children were in bed, the husband said, "I passed Mr. Scrooge's office today. His partner, Mr. Marley, is near death, and Scrooge sat there all alone. I doubt he has a friend in the world."

Scrooge turned to the spirit and cried, "Remove me from this place! Haunt me no longer!" Suddenly he realized that he was back in his own room. He gave a sigh of relief and fell asleep at once.

Later that night, Scrooge awoke in the middle of a particularly loud snore. He heard the clock strike, but no ghost appeared. Instead a strange light came from the next room. He opened the door and saw a jolly giant, surrounded by delicious food and drink.

"I am the Ghost of Christmas Present," said the spirit. "Touch my robe, and come with me."

Scrooge touched the spirit's robe and found that he was floating through the streets on Christmas morning. Before long they were inside Bob Cratchit's house. The door opened, and Bob entered carrying his youngest child, Tiny Tim, on his shoulders. In the boy's hand was the crutch he needed in order to walk. In spite of his poor health, Tiny Tim was always cheerful.

"And how did Tiny Tim behave in church?" asked
Mrs. Cratchit.

"As good as gold!" replied Bob.

They sat down at the table and carved a small roast
goose. Then came Christmas pudding, roasted
chestnuts, and Christmas punch. Bob held up his glass
and said, "Merry Christmas to us all. God bless us!"

"God bless us, every one," echoed Tiny Tim.

Scrooge looked at the spirit and asked, "Will the boy live?"

The spirit answered, "I see a vacant seat in the chimney corner, and a crutch without an owner. If these shadows remain unaltered by the future, the child will die."

"No, spirit!" cried Scrooge. "Spare him, please!"

But the spirit said, "If he is going to die, he had better do it and decrease the surplus population." Scrooge realized that these words were his own, and he hung his head in shame.

Suddenly Bob held up his glass again and cried, "I give you Mr. Scrooge—the founder of the feast!"

"The founder of the feast indeed!" cried Mrs. Cratchit. "I wish I had him here—the stingy, unfeeling man! I'd give him a piece of my mind to feast upon!"

"My dear," said her husband. "The children! Christmas day!"

Scrooge was saddened to see that the very mention of his name brought a dark cloud over the gathering. But in a few minutes it passed, and the entire family was even merrier than before.

By now, the streets were full of people on their way to visit friends and relatives. A fire blazed in every fireplace, and the joy of Christmas was in every heart.

The spirit led Scrooge to his nephew's house, where a party was being held. The nephew laughed heartily as he said, "My Uncle Scrooge is a strange old fellow. As rich as he is, his money does him no good. And he's such an old grouch that he even refuses to come to dinner! So whom does he hurt? Himself! I'm sure he will pay dearly for being so unpleasant, so I will say nothing against him. In fact, I'll drink to his health. Merry Christmas and a Happy New Year to old Uncle Scrooge!"

Presently the spirit turned to Scrooge and said, "My time here will soon end. But before I go, there is something else you must see." Then he showed Scrooge two ragged, half-starved children.

"Oh spirit," cried Scrooge, "is there no way to help them? Is there no place for the needy to go?"

The spirit replied, "Are there no prisons? Are there no workhouses?" Then the bells began to toll, and the spirit disappeared.

At the final stroke, another spirit approached, moving like a phantom from the grave. It said nothing, and Scrooge could see no face beneath its hooded robe.

"Are you the Ghost of Christmas Yet to Come?" asked Scrooge. There was no answer. Scrooge cried out, "I fear you more than any specter I have yet seen." The ghost said nothing, but led him into the city. There, they overheard some merchants talking about someone who had died.

"I don't know anyone who'll go to his funeral," said one. "He didn't have a single friend that I know of."

"It'll be a cheap funeral, no doubt," said the other, laughing.

Just then, two wealthy businessmen came down the street. Scrooge recognized them, for he had dealt with them in his business. "Well," said the first, "Old Scratch has finally died." And the second replied, "So I am told. Quite cold this evening, isn't it?" And they walked on without another word.

The spirit took Scrooge to a dreary shop where secondhand things were bought and sold. Some disreputable characters had spread out the things they had stolen from the dead man.

"He won't be needing these anymore," cackled a woman, holding up the dead man's bed curtains. Then she took a fine shirt out of her bag. "And they were going to bury him in *this*," she said. "It's too good to waste on a dead man, so I took it off him!" And she cackled even louder.

Suddenly Scrooge jumped back, for the scene had changed, and he now found himself next to a bed on which the dead man lay. He could not find the courage to peek under the sheet and see who it was. Instead, he said to the spirit, "If there is any person in the town who feels emotion caused by this man's death, then show that person to me."

At once Scrooge looked in upon a small room. As a man came in, his wife asked hopefully, "Did he give us more time to pay off the loan?"

"He did not," said her husband. "They tell me he is dead."

The woman was relieved and happy. "Then we shall have a bit more time," she said, "for no one could be so merciless a creditor as he."

"Spirit," pleaded Scrooge, "let me see some tenderness connected with a death." The phantom took him to the Cratchit house, where everyone sat around the table. But Tiny Tim was not there. His crutch leaned against the corner.

"I saw Mr. Scrooge's nephew today," said Bob. "He told me he was sorry to hear that our Tim had died." At the mention of Tiny Tim's name, Mrs. Cratchit's eyes filled with tears, and Bob took her hand to comfort her. Then he said, "He told me to call on him if he could help us. It seemed almost as if he had known our Tim and could feel our sorrow with us."

A moment later, Scrooge found himself in a cemetery, where the specter pointed to a gravestone. "Tell me, spirit," said Scrooge, "are these the shadows of things that *will* be, or the shadows of things that *may* be?"

The ghost did not answer, but pointed to the grave.

On the gravestone was the name EBENEZER SCROOGE.

Scrooge fell to his knees, crying, "Am *I* that man who lay upon the bed? Oh spirit, say that I can change these shadows! I will honor Christmas in my heart, and keep it all the year. Just tell me that this need not be so!" But the phantom shriveled and shrank until it was nothing but the bedpost in Scrooge's room.

Scrooge jumped out of bed and leaned out the window. "What day is it?" he called to a boy on the street below. The boy replied that it was Christmas day. Scrooge began dancing with joy. "Is that prize turkey still hanging in the window of the shop down the street?" he asked. It was. "Excellent!" chuckled Scrooge.

Then he tossed down some money to the boy and said, "Buy that turkey and take it to Bob Cratchit's house! But don't tell him who sent it. Be quick about it, and you can keep the change! Merry Christmas!"

A few minutes later, Scrooge was dressed and walking down the street. The first person he met was the fat gentleman who had asked for a donation the day before. Scrooge greeted him with a hearty "Merry Christmas," and then whispered something in the man's ear.

"My dear Mr. Scrooge, how very generous of you!" exclaimed the man. "I don't know what to say!"

"Don't say anything," chuckled Scrooge. "I'll have a check drawn up tomorrow. Just stop by my office and pick it up." Then he walked through the city, greeting everyone with a warm smile and a pleasant "Merry Christmas!"

By dinner time, he had arrived at his nephew's house. He passed the door a dozen times before he had the courage to knock.

"Well, bless my soul!" exclaimed Scrooge's nephew. "Merry Christmas, Uncle! Come in! Come in and join the fun!" Scrooge stayed for dinner and never enjoyed a meal so much. And when they played games and danced, Scrooge joined right in with the other guests. It was the merriest Christmas he had ever had!

The next day, Scrooge was waiting when Bob Cratchit came into the office. "Cratchit!" he growled in his meanest voice. "You're late!"

"I'm sorry, sir," said Bob. "It won't happen again."

"Now see here," growled Scrooge, "I'm not going to stand for this any longer! And therefore," he continued, poking his clerk in the ribs and smiling, "I'm going to raise your salary!"

Bob hardly knew what to say. "Are you feeling all right, Mr. Scrooge?" he asked.

"I feel wonderful!" said Scrooge. "Merry Christmas, my boy! I'll raise your salary, and I'll do whatever I can to help your family. Now, throw some more coal on that fire. It's too chilly in here for a man to be comfortable!"

As it happened, Scrooge was better than his word. He became a good friend and a good employer. He became like a second father to Tiny Tim, who did not die after all. And from that day forth, it was always said that Ebenezer Scrooge certainly knew the real meaning of Christmas.